A

Robert Cloudy wa
mining town of Ba
the outskirts of towi
, ~ ~... and Diane, with
older brother, Dean, and older sister, Donna. Robert
enjoyed a fruitful childhood and a lust for life which
sometimes led to mischief and mayhem. Robert was
not an academic child, but he was most certainly a
dreamer! Telling stories wherever he went, he would
one day dream of being an actor, but sadly this was
not going to be Robert's path. For much of Robert's
childhood and early adult life, Robert felt too much
of a pull to normality and a mundane existence, while
there is certainly nothing wrong with this, Robert
wanted more, he wanted to be creative, to entertain.
Robert drifted from job to job, dreaming of what could
have been. After meeting a friend of his wife well into
his thirties, he realised dreams can be caught. Now,
the sky is the limit for Robert, wait, no, there are NO
limits for Robert and his bright future.

Winter Mouse was originally drafted in the winter of
2015 but lay on a pile of papers on Robert Cloudy's
desk. After the death of his aunt, Robert played a pre-
recorded version to his cousin Gavin. With Gavin
and his immediate family's encouragement, Robert
decided to take the plunge. It was a chain of events
that led Robert to approach publishers to have *Winter
Mouse* brought to life.

Winter Mouse
A Christmas Tale

Robert Cloudy

Winter Mouse
A Christmas Tale

Nightingale Books

A CIP catalogue record for this title is
available from the British Library.
ISBN 9781838751050

*Nightingale Books is an imprint of
Pegasus Elliot MacKenzie Publishers Ltd.
www.pegasuspublishers.com*

First Published in 2021

Nightingale Books
Sheraton House Castle Park
Cambridge England

Printed & Bound in Great Britain

Dedication

This book is dedicated to Jackie Smith.

Thank you for everything Jackie.

Acknowledgements

I would like to thank my dad for all of the advice that he used to give me whilst growing up, helping me stand tall and to fight for what I believe in. I would like to thank my mum for the love and support throughout my life, I truly could not have wished for a better mum. To my wife, Nichola. You never gave up on me when things got tough, I would absolutely never have achieved so much without you by my side. To my many friends and family, I could not have achieved this feat without your support and encouragement. To Lisa Walker of White Apple Thinking, your wisdom is beyond belief and you helped me to believe in myself and led me into a great mental space in order to achieve this and so many other goals. And finally, and by no means least, to my two children, Oliver and Annabelle. You are the two best things in my life and this book is for the two of you. Making you both proud is what keeps me going in life. Dream your dreams for now little ones, for when you grow, I know for sure, those dreams will come true.

Once upon a time there lived a mouse called Winter.

A mouse is usually a fun little animal, the heart and soul of the party one would say, but not Winter, Winter was a grumpy little mouse, he didn't have many friends, well, not really, none at all.

Winter's story begins one Christmas many years ago when Winter was just a child, he had asked Santa for an unusual gift that year. What Winter wanted was no ordinary present for a child, what he wanted more then anything else was a lovely cheese board.

Winter wanted to have the best Christmas ever and wanted to share the cheese with his mum, dad and baby sister.

Christmas was a very special time of the year and Winter wanted his family to eat like kings and for once not have to eat the scraps pillaged from the wheelie bins in the farmer's yard.

"Not tonight! Not this Christmas!" Winter wailed. "I just want to treat my family to one day of bliss, even if it is just for one day!"

That night, that Christmas eve, the snow fell and fell and fell. Winter watched from his bedroom window, the snow kept on falling,

until there was nothing, nothing but white and blackness.

Winter's mum and dad came in to his room.

"We need to check the food stores!" his dad said. "Watch your sister until we return," he requested.

Winter thought nothing of this as during a storm of any kind his parents would check on the food supply. Winter smiled and nodded then turned back to watch the snow falling past the window once again.

After a short while Winter yawned and decided to get in bed and go to sleep, his mum and dad had not yet returned but winter knew his sister Jessica would come to his room if she needed anything. Winter switched off his bedside lamp and rolled onto his side and went to sleep.

The next morning, Winter woke to the faint tugging of his ear, Winter turned over to see a very agitated Jessica.

"What's wrong? Where are Mum and Dad?" Winter asked.

"They are gone, they are not in the house," Jessica said.

Winter paused for a moment. "They went to check on the food stores last night, did they not come back?" Winter asked.

Jessica did not reply to this, her face said it all. Winter realised something was not quite right and he jumped out of bed and began to quickly get dressed.

"It will be fine, Jessica!" Winter said as he slung on his coat. Winter knew something was wrong of course, he could tell his sister was worried so he tried to offer her reassurance. Jessica ran to get dressed too, as she reached for her coat from her closet Winter cut her off.

"No, Jessica, you stay here it may not be safe, and besides someone needs to watch the house in case they come back."

Jessica reluctantly agreed and retreated to the window and looked out of it. Winter opened the front door and quickly scurried through it.

Outside the house the snow covered almost everything, Winter stopped in his tracks and let out a large gasp, all that Winter could see was a few trees and the smoke from the chimneys of the houses in the distance. No paw prints or tracks, absolutely nothing.

Winter checked with the local birds, he spoke with a robin called Gabriel but he nor any of the birds had seen anyone and Gabriel had been up since dawn.

Winter also passed his neighbour David the hare. "Have you seen my mum and dad?" Winter asked.

"I'm very sorry, Winter, I haven't seen anyone today," David said. "I hope you find them."

At this point Winter was getting worried. He arrived at the food store, it was fine, nothing had been touched. I better get back, Jessica will be worried too, Winter thought to himself.

Winter returned home as quickly as he could, Jessica was in her bedroom sobbing into her blanket. Winter tried to reassure her.

"It will be fine Jessica," he said. "They will come back."

Jessica stayed in her room the whole day, she was too upset to come out. Winter cooked a Christmas dinner for the two of them while they waited. And waited. Minutes became hours, hours became days. Weeks, months, years passed.

Jessica never gave up hope, she always believed that one day Mum and Dad would return. It was a very different story for Winter, he became angry and irritable, he blamed himself of course.

After several years Jessica decided to move out of their home. By this point Winter had closed himself off from all of his friends and from her too. She wanted to start a family so that is exactly what she did. From then on Winter lived alone.

Winter hated Christmas, all Christmas did for him now, was remind him of the night his parents did not come home. It was also the day that Winter stopped believing in Santa.

So, Winter would never celebrate Christmas, he would ignore his sister's invites to join her with her new family, he would just sit in his chair with a glass of milk and do crosswords. And that is exactly how it would be for Winter, until…tonight, Christmas eve, thirty years to the very night he lost his parents.

Winter was cooking in the kitchen when he noticed a blizzard outside his window. Much like the one thirty years prior.

Worrying he had not locked them up, Winter grabbed his coat and walking stick and went to check on his food stores. Winter arrived at the stores and made sure all of his food was secure.

By this point the blizzard was getting worse, Winter was struggling to see much further then ten feet in front of him. I better get home Winter thought to himself.

On his way home he noticed a faint light in the distance, the light began to shine brighter. Now the light was accompanied by a noise of some kind.

As the noise grew louder it became clearer, it was like some sort of animal, in fact several animals.

Winter began to shiver with fear. He quickly hid behind an old fence and waited. Pretty soon the noise and light were almost upon him, growing louder and louder. Then, the noise came almost to a halt, there was somebody there.

After a short pause, Winter plucked up the courage to peep over the fence. There, in the shadows stood a man dressed in red and white, he had silvery white hair with a large bushy beard and enormous bushy eyebrows. Behind him stood eight reindeer with a huge sled in tow, the light Winter had seen was from a solitary lantern upon the sled.

The man peered down on Winter. "You there," the man gently whispered. Winter steadily walked from behind the fence

"I suppose you are Santa Claus?" Winter cleverly muttered.

"Why yes, I am. Santa Claus at your service!" the man said. "Are you a non believer?"

"Yes. I most certainly am a non believer!" Winter said. Then Winter paused for a moment. Winter's eyes widened as he began to speak again, "OK, I have an idea! Prove it to me. Prove you are Santa Claus. I bet you can't.

"OK then," the man said as he chuckled and turned to his sled. "By the way," the man said as he turned back to Winter, "it's Winter isn't it?"

Winter was astonished by this. How does he know my name? Winter thought to himself. Then, before Winter could ask the man how he knew him, the man pulled out a huge list of people and several opened letters. Winter recognised them, they were his. Winter had written to Santa every year but had not received a present in longer than he could remember.

"I am so sorry, Winter," Santa Claus said.

"Sorry? What for?" Winter asked.

"Why, for being late of course!" the man said as he started to pull present after present off his sled. "These are your presents," the man said, "all of them. One for every Christmas I have missed."

Winter was shocked. "They're all here, all of them!" he said. "A bike, a toy car, a slide. Wow, you really do exist!" Winter said.

The man chuckled for a moment. "Well of course I exist!" Santa said.

Santa explained that years and years ago he had lost the directions to Winter's house and every year he brought all of Winter's presents along in an attempt to retrace his steps in the hope of finding him. Every year he had failed, until this year. Winter was amazed.

"Here, Winter," Santa said as he leaned over towards him with one more present. "This present is a special present, by way of an apology."

Winter looked up at Santa for a moment, then tore off the wrapping. "An alarm clock?" a puzzled Winter said.

"Yes!" said Santa, "it is no ordinary alarm clock however, take it straight home and set it for the morning."

"But why?" Winter asked. Winter was intrigued.

"Please, Winter, just do as I say!" Santa requested.

"OK, Santa, I will!" Winter turned to scurry back home. Winter stopped and turned back to Santa. "Oh, and, Santa, I'm sorry for not believing."

"That's OK, Winter," said Santa.

And in that moment Santa hopped back on his sled and grabbed the reins.

"Where are you going?" Winter asked.

Santa smiled, "I can't stay around chatting all night, I have a job to do remember?"

Winter grinned, then nodded and waved as Santa sat down. Before Winter could speak again the sled kicked into action and up into the sky it went, off into the night.

As soon as Santa had gone Winter ran home with the mystic alarm clock that he had just been given.

He went straight up to his room and set the alarm for first thing the next morning. Winter got straight into his pyjamas and snuggled up in his match box bed.

The next morning arrived and the alarm clock woke Winter up as expected. Winter rubbed his eyes and got out of bed and went downstairs in his usual dazed state. Winter walked into the kitchen to get some breakfast and there, to his amazement stood his mum and dad.

Winter rubbed his eyes in disbelief. "MUM, DAD!" Winter screamed. "You're both here." Winter ran to them and threw his arms round them.

"Why of course we are, are you alright?" His mum asked. At that moment, Winter heard another voice.

"Have you fallen out of bed onto your head again?" The voice said. After a moment Winter realised who the voice belonged to, it was Jessica's voice. As Winter turned around his jaw dropped, Jessica was a child again, he looked into a mirror and noticed he was also a child again. Then, Winter noticed that the house was different somehow. Winter paused for a moment.

"Wait a minute!" Winter said as his eyes lit up. "The ALARM CLOCK!" Winter shouted as he ran out of the kitchen and up the stairs to his room.

Winter's mum, dad and Jessica all quickly followed, purely out of interest at what was going on. When Winter got to his room he started to search, his bedside table, the closet, his sock drawer and under the bed... nothing.

"Its not here!" he said with a dejected expression.

"What son? What's not here?" his dad asked.

Winter explained what had happened the night before and what had happened all those years ago when they had gone missing. Winter's mum threw her arms around Winter.

It was just a dream she said as she kissed Winter on his forehead. Winter agreed that this could be the only explanation. Then at that very moment Winter looked out of his bedroom window and noticed some faint sled marks in the fresh snow below, and right by the marks there was a large cheeseboard with a bow around it. Winter paused for a moment, his eyes opened wide as he noticed the cheeseboard.

Or was it a dream?

Winter smiled.

The End